VISITING
Day

BY JACQUELINE WOODSON

ILLUSTRATED BY JAMES E. RANSOME

PUFFIN BOOKS
An Imprint of Penguin Group (USA)

ONLY ON VISITING DAY
is there chicken frying
in the kitchen at 6 A.M.
and Grandma
humming soft and low,
smiling her secret
just-for-Daddy-and-me smile,

and me lying in bed,
smiling my just-for-Grandma-and-Daddy smile.

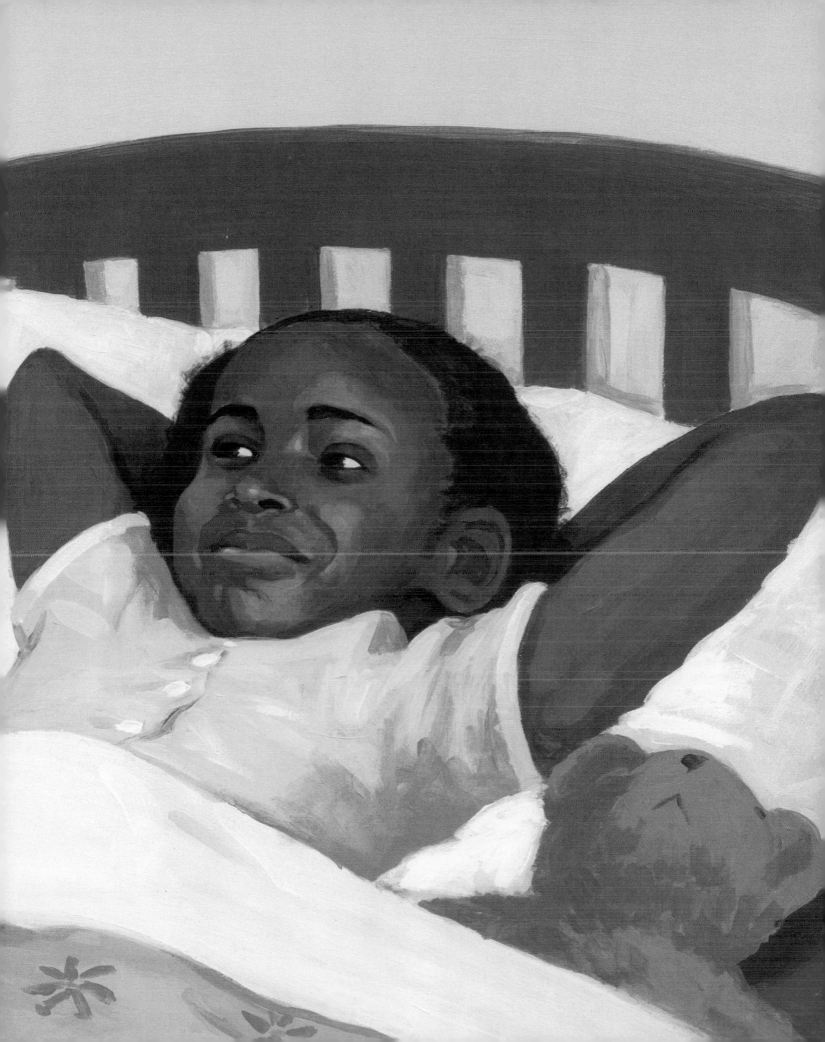

And maybe Daddy is
already up,
brushing his teeth,
combing his hair back, saying,
"Yeah, that pretty little girl of mine is coming today,"
with all the men around him
looking on jealous-like
'cause they wish they had
a little girl of their own coming.

Only on Visiting Day
does Mrs. Tate come over
when the sky is still pink,
heavy with presents for her
son, Thomas, saying,
"Please, can you take these with you?"
and Grandma taking the presents from
Mrs. Tate's arms,

and shooting me a look that says, "You better not make a sound about Mrs. Tate not having money to take the bus up there to see her only son."

And I sit quiet, respectful.

Only on Visiting Day
do I stand patiently at the bus stop,
holding tight to Grandma's hand
until everybody's inside.

but instead, I go to sleep
and don't wake up again
until the bus pulls up in front
of the big old building
where, as Grandma puts it,
Daddy is doing a little time.

And only on Visiting Day do I get to tell Daddy
everything that has happened over the month,
while I sit in his lap and he pulls on my braids,
smiling his big
me-and-Grandma-have-been-gone-forever smile,
laughing his big laugh,
showing me and Grandma off to his friends,
pressing peppermints into my hand
and kisses against
Grandma's cheek.

Grandma says it's not forever going to be like this.

She says, one day,
we'll be able to wake up
and have Daddy right there in our house again,
and we won't have to take long bus rides once a month
and walk home from the bus stop hand in hand,
feeling a little sad,
already starting to miss Daddy.

Grandma says all it takes is time,
a little time,
and while we're holding out waiting
for Daddy to come home
we can count our blessings
and love each other up
and make biscuits and cakes
and pretty pictures to send Daddy . . .

And in the early evening,
if it's a little chilly outside,
we can sit out back
bundled up in blankets
and make each other laugh
as we make big plans
for when Daddy comes home again.

In memory of my uncle Robert Leon Irby and my grandmother, Georgianna Scott Irby—J.W.

for J.E. Williams—J.E.R.

AUTHOR'S NOTE

When I was growing up, I had a favorite uncle. My mother's brother, Robert, was the best dancer in our family. He was funny and handsome and always came to our house with surprising gifts for me—a doll whose hair grew, a pair of skates, a new record that he'd teach me all the words to, a joke I could actually understand—all kinds of things. But my uncle Robert went to prison when I was very young. I never knew what his crime was and it really didn't matter. I knew I loved him dearly and he loved me with the same ferocity. I knew that some of my happiest moments in childhood were spent getting on that bus to go visit him, climbing off hours later and walking through the many steel doors that led to where my uncle was waiting, his hair brushed, his prison uniform cleaned and pressed, his smile brighter than anything. As he laughed and talked with me and my family, I forgot, for the moment, where we were. I knew we were a family. I knew we were happy. I knew there was lots of love in the room. And on those trips home, I knew there was a sadness surrounding us. And a hope—that one day there wouldn't be prison walls. That one day my uncle would be free.

Although VISITING DAY is a work of fiction, it is based on true events from my childhood. The dad in VISITING DAY is a lot like my uncle. The grandmother—a lot like my own grandmother.

My uncle died at a young age two years ago. When he died, he'd been free from prison for a long time. Only a little over a year later, my grandmother passed away. I dedicate this book to both of them. I am glad I have the memories of my uncle as a free man. But I am also grateful for those visiting day memories—waking up before dawn to my grandmother frying chicken and making lunch and dinner for us and those long, slow afternoons when my family sat with my uncle, laughing and telling stories and loving each other up.

I am grateful to James Ransome for his amazing talent as an artist, for making this book whole and beautiful. I am grateful to my uncle and grandmother for giving me this story to tell. And I am grateful to the universe for the gift to tell it well.

ARTIST'S NOTE

When I first received and read Jackie's text for VISITING DAY, it stopped me cold. I sat down to gather my thoughts. The story was beautiful, powerful, and emotional, obviously the work of a sensitive artist.

First, I thought how fortunate I was to have the opportunity to create images that would accompany this text. Next, I wondered if I had told Jackie about what was going on in my own family; if this was the reason she had asked her editor to send me the story. After all, my brother being incarcerated was a family secret, something we could only whisper about. I could not help but be concerned for my nephews who were in the same position as the little girl in this story. I questioned whether or not we should shed light on such a controversial issue. On the other hand it was a subject that kids across the country were dealing with every day, and I felt comforted that Jackie was also working from her own personal experiences with visiting days.

I had only one visiting day with my brother. The trip was of course very emotional for the two of us, but as usual we covered it with smiles and laughter. It is from that visit that I pull my images for the illustrations in the story. I will never forget the contrast of the clear blue sky, and the pure green grass against the cold brick building with black windows that housed him, and the barbed wire fence that separated us for all those months.

Finally, I realized I had never spoken to Jackie or anyone else outside my immediate family about my brother's situation. They say that the right stories often find you, and this is an example of how one story found me.

PUFFIN BOOKS Published by the Penguin Group Penguin Group (USA) LLC 375 Hudson Street New York, New York 10014 USA * Canada * UK * Ireland * Australia * New Zealand * India * South Africa * China • penguin.com A Penguin Random House Company • First published in the United States of America by Scholastic Press, an imprint of Scholastic Inc., 2002 • Published by Puffin Books, an imprint of Penguin Young Readers Group, 2015 • Text copyright © 2002 by Jacqueline Woodson • Illustrations copyright © 2002 by James E. Ransome • Penguin supports copyright. Copyright fuels creativity, encourages diverse voices, promotes free speech, and creates a vibrant culture. Thank you for buying an authorized edition of this book and for complying with copyright laws by not reproducing, scanning, or distributing any part of it in any form without permission. You are supporting writers and allowing Penguin to continue to publish books for every reader. • THE LIBRARY OF CONGRESS HAS CATALOGED THE SCHOLASTIC PRESS EDITION AS FOLLOWS: • Woodson, Jacqueline. Visiting Day / by Jacqueline Woodson; illustrated by James E. Ransome.—1st ed. p. cm. • Summary: A young girl and her grandmother visit the girl's father in prison. • ISBN: 0-590-40005-3 (hc) [1. Prisons—Fiction. 2. Prisoners—Fiction. 3. Fathers and daughters—Fiction. 4. Grandmothers—Fiction. 5. Afro-Americans—Fiction.] I. Ransome, James E. ill. II. Title. PZ7.W868 Vi 2001 [E]—dc21 00-035772 Puffin Books ISBN 978-0-14-751608-4 • James E. Ransome's paintings are rendered in acrylic. Maya's art on the back cover is rendered in crayon. Manufactured in China